PREMISE

Throughout U.S. American History racism has played a key role in society. Often when we as a nation discuss slavery, it is from one point of view. The view is either as a black person telling their story of slavery from their thoughts as a Slave or as a white person doing the same as a Master. What I would like for everyone to do is look at slavery as if the white man is the Slave and the black man is the Master.

WHAT IF

PROLOGUE

Everybody will look at things from their own perspective. Most of these perspectives really come from the values that were passed on to them from family members. As a child you formulate the way you should walk and talk as you watch and interact with parents and other family members. The traditions and cultural values that are presented to you become your initial values. Historically, American white children were raised to believe they were the superior race and African Americans were seen as a lower class of people. White Americans were privileged with better school conditions. They had books and that gave them an advantage over black Americans who had to use the hand me downs white Americans no longer needed. Black American children were taught by their parents' example that they

WHAT IF

A Walk through Time

Everyone should ask themselves that question!

James HTOWN
Horton

had to work twice as hard as the white children in order to be successful only to have their ideas and creative work stolen from them.

Professor Kevin Francis stood 5'9 and weighed a chiseled 182 pounds, and sported a cleaned shaved bald head. His glasses were wire framed with rounded lenses that reminded me of the ones that Gandhi wore. As Professor Francis articulated his words you would have thought he was a Harvard grad; but no, he graduated from Howard. Kevin was top of his class, received scholarships and was the first in his family to graduate from college.

Kevin grew up in North East Houston and attended Nimitz Senior High school. He was in the honor society and played the clarinet. When he got out of daily band practice, Kevin would go home and pick up his lawn mower for his afternoon grass cutting job. Every day his little brother Jamal would sit on the steps or the curb completing his homework. This was their time to talk, practice math questions and study for Jamal's vocabulary test. Once Kevin completed the yards, they had to hurry home to complete their daily chores. Kevin had to be a father figure for his younger brother as they lost their father to a railroad accident. Mrs. Francis worked two jobs to make ends meet and was barely getting by each month. The extra money that Kevin made was used for the clothing they got from Good Will and for additional school supplies. They were a tight knit family and were very thankful for all they had.

During the month of February the Professor had a tradition of starting the class off with African American facts, but today was different. It was March 1st. On this day in 1927, Harry Belafonte was born. He was a singer and actor who...........

"Excuse me Professor, Excuse me!" exclaimed Edward. "Today is March 1st and why are you giving the class African American history facts in the month of March? Don't you think one month is enough to celebrate your history?"

Edward Langston III stood at 6'1 with an athletic build. His hair was smooth, jet black and laid flat. Edward spoke with an upstate English accent that was part New York and part Connecticut. Edward's father was a retired Navy Admiral who served 35 years on active service. Edward was the elder of three siblings named Jason, Adam and Merry, all of who attended private schools in Connecticut.

Edward graduated high school with a 3.1 GPA. He was the Captain of the Lacrosse team, but lost that position due to a drinking and driving charge. The Judge who presided over the case reduced the charge to underage drinking and gave Edward 20 hours of community of service as a favor to his friend the Admiral. Harvard Admissions did not want to let Edward enroll, but his father was part of the alumni. The Admiral called in another favor and his son was admitted into Harvard.

Professor Francis acknowledged Edward and gave him a nice smile. "Mr.Langston, thanks for today's update. I am very impressed that you can read a calendar as you can never seem to get the exam dates right."

Laughter could be heard from the class.

"Well Professor, I don't see the point of discussing African American History in this class. We all know what happened in the past, so let's just keep the past in the past. Everyone is treated the same now, and if you ask me this country has given the blacks in this country so much."

"Well Mr. Langston, let me ask you this one question!"

WHAT IF

ACT I

CHAPTER ONE

THE AWAKENING 1725

"What the Hell is that smell? Where am I? Where are my clothes?"

"Keep quiet! Keep quiet, or you gonna get us in trouble," replied Jason.

"Oh my God what is that smell? It smells like rotting flesh and urine!"

Edward looked around the room he saw a door that had an opening, but it had bars. The floor that he was lying on was a brownish tan dirt color. To the far right side of the room where the smell was coming from, Edward could see buckets filled with feces and other body fluids.

"Where in the hell am I?"

"Edward, calm down! Calm down," whispered Jason." If you keep up the noise then you will get all of us in trouble."

"Jason who are all these people and where are we? Why are Merry and Adam lying on this dirt floor crying and how did we get here? Jason explain please! Please explain!" begged Edward.

"Quiet down in there, you Niggers, or else your flesh will taste the end of my whip."

"Who is that Jason? What are they talking about? It is only white people in here." Jason began to tell Edward that they are in a room waiting to be auctioned off to the highest bidder.

"What do you mean? How can that be? I thought slavery was over, and why are we the ones being sold?"

"Guard, come here now. I demand answers. My name is Edward Langston III and you will give me answers right now."

"Ha, Ha, Ha. Demand answers!" More laughter continued. "If you want answers, then answers you shall have. (The crack of a whip sound began: Wuh-PSSSH Wuh-PSSSH Wuh-PSSSH.)

Everyone except Edward began to huddle on one side of the room, not making a sound. The latch bolt on the door unlocked, and boom! The door swung open. Five black men of average build emerged with night sticks, with a sixth black man who was heavy set with a rounded belly. It was obvious he didn't miss a meal. He was carrying a long black whip that resembled the color and shape of a black racer snake with the end of the whip flared out into five little fingers.

"My name is Edward." Immediately, the five men began to rush toward Edward and started beating him down. They subdued Edward and tied him to the pole next to the nauseating smell coming from the room.

"So, you are the Nigger causing all of this noise,"

5

stated the Collector.

"You can't do this to me!" exclaimed Edward.

"Well, you demanded answers and now you shall have them." Wuh-PSSSH! Wuh-PSSSH! Wuh-PSSSH Wuh-PSSSH! Wuh-PSSSH! "Now, do you demand any more answers?" asked the Collector. "I am more than glad to answer your questions."

Edward just laid there tied to the pole and whimpered. The smell that he woke up to now was nonexistent. The shirt that he was wearing was now ripped, and everywhere the black racer had made contact you could see five little red fingers. "Keep quiet or else I will be back to have another discussion with you," replied the Collector. The Collector and the guards left the room.

Jason, Merry and Adam came over and untied their brother. "Just lie here and keep quiet," stated Jason. Edward prayed and whimpered himself to sleep.

CHAPTER TWO

AUCTION AND SEPARATION

"Today I bring to you one of the best looking stock I have seen in my last 3 years. I have a family of three bull Niggers that will make good field hands and produce good offspring. When we conclude this auction, someone will be taking home the prize of the day. I have a healthy female heifer Nigger whose rose has never been plucked and this Nigger could be used for cooking, cleaning and whatever else is needed."

"Come here boy. Open your mouth. Teeth look ok for a nigger. What's your name?"

"My name is Edward Langston III."

"WHAT? My name is Edward Langston III. Who

do you think you are; a special kind of Nigger?"

"No, but my name is Edward Langston III."

"Nope. From this day forward, your name will be Rayquan and you will address me as Mr. Jackson."

"My name is Edward Langston III."

"Mr. Collector, I will take this Nigger and his little sister. I am going to love breaking this one right here."

"What about my brothers?" exclaimed Rayquan.

SWAT!! "Shut up and only speak when spoken to."

"Mr. Collector, I don't want the other two scrawny niggers. Send them to my brother in Arkansas and I will take these two to the Bayou in Louisiana."

"Please, please, please don't separate us. Jason, Jason I will find you and Adam."

SWAT!! SWAT!! "I told you not to speak." SWAT! SWAT!

CHAPTER THREE

WELCOME HOME

Wuh-PSSSH Wuh-PSSSH Wuh-PSSSH.

"Alright you new Niggers, this is your new home. You have just arrived at the Jackson plantation. When I come around, you will greet me with a Good morning, Good afternoon, or Good evening, Mr. Omar Johnson. Anything outside of that will be met with a slow and educating lashing. Only my friends can call me OJ. Master Jackson tells me that I have a special Nigger here in the bunch. Which one of y'all boys is Edward Langston III? "

"I am right here Mr. Johnson." Wuh-PSSSH! Wuh-PSSSH!

"Yea Boy. Master Jackson was right. You think you are special. You're a special kind of stupid, aren't you boy? D'ante get your white ass over here."

"Good afternoon Mr. Johnson."

"Master Jackson tells me that this nigger name is Rayquan but he thinks his name is Edward Langston III. What do you think I should do about this?"

"Mr. Johnson, he needs one of your education sessions. Should me and Roman prepare him for your teaching?"

Wuh-PSSSH! Wuh-PSSSH!

"D'ante you my Nigger! My Nigger! Get Mr. Langston as he calls himself ready. We gonna hold us a class today."

"Yes sir, Boss. Yes sir. He needs to know his name."

"Now, Rayquan, the first thing I told you to do was to greet me first, but you chose to ignore that. The second thing is, you think that your name is Edward Langston III. Master Jackson gave you the name of Rayquan, but you chose to ignore that. I will be giving you 15 lashes for not greeting me and D'ante will give you a minimum of ten or more until you learn your name. When I am done giving you today's teaching, your sister Porsche will massage my arm while D'ante continues to educate you."

CHAPTER FOUR

CHICKEN COOP

"Kelly, Kelly where is that Nigger girl you promised me?" yelled Mrs. Jackson.

"She better know how to clean and wax floors better than the last one you gave me. D'ante, get that little Nigger girl to me now and you best be quick about it."

As Porsche begin to walk she saw a huge white home. She thought to herself that this had to be the best home she had ever seen. The house was two stories tall and had eight marble columns with the initials KJ in a circle on the four columns in the center of the home. The handrails were made of cast iron and had a smooth black paint finish. Each window had flat black paneling on the outside but with pure white curtains that opened in a reverse letter V shape. In the middle of the column stood a beautiful, pecan tan woman. Mrs. Jackson had an impressive hour glass shape and her hair was silky black.

"What yo name is girl?"

"Good afternoon Mrs. Jackson, my name is Porsche."

"You sure is one young funny looking and smelling one. You best to get yourself cleaned up because you want be stinking up my home. Go ahead and take off those rags. Susan, bring over the soap and that wash pan."

Porsche stood about 5'5 with sandy brown hair and blue eyes. Her face was rounded with strong cheekbones and she had a dimple on her chin. The frame of her body resembled that of a volleyball player. Porsche's breasts were firm and they sat up nice and perky.

All the field hands and Mr. Jackson begin to watch as the water was poured on Porsche and Susan began to wash her.

"Wanda! What the hell are you doing to that girl?" yelled Mr. Jackson.

"You better not damage our new property. I spent good money on that one and I have special plans for her."

"I don't want no stinky dirty heifer coming into my house. This is my Nigger and I will do whatever I want with her. You just worry about those field Niggers and leave the house ones to me."

"You do want dinner tonight," replied Mrs. Jackson as she turned and walked back into the home.

"Alright, Alright, you Niggers. Get your eyes off of that heifer and back to work. Your show is over." Edward knew the show was not over. He could see that in Mr. Jackson eyes.

"O.J, man did you see how nice of a body Porsche had on her yesterday?"

"Yes I did Mr. Jackson and it is very nice for a white

nigger."

"Well, you make sure nobody, and I mean nobody, lay a hand on her. I have plans for that one. Do you understand me O.J?"

"Yes Mr. Jackson! When Shall I make the arrangements for you to see her?"

"Have her bring me two glasses of lemonade around noon and I will take it from there."

"Good afternoon, Mr. Jackson. I have your lemonade as you requested. Is there anything else I can do for you?"

"As a matter of fact, yes there is. Go ahead and enjoy that other glass of lemonade. Tonight when I go for my evening walk around I want you to meet me by the chicken coop."

"Sir, why? Did I do something wrong?"

"Porsche, do you know why I purchased you? "

"No Sir."

"Well, you know I purchased you and you are my property. That means I can do whatever I want with you. You will not ask me why. Do as I tell you. Do you understand me? You will be there and wait for me. You will not tell anyone about our meeting. I will see you tonight."

"Yes Sir." Porsche understood that now was not the time to ask questions. Whatever Mr. Jackson wanted, Mr. Jackson got. She got the feeling that that if she did not do as requested she would get the same as her brother Raquan.

As the sun started to set, Raquan could see Porsche was distracted and nervous. He had not seen that look since the day he woke up on that dirt floor. Porsche was only 15 and nobody was going to hurt his little sister. He would rather die before he let any harm come to her.

"Porsche, what's wrong? You seem upset. Did that mean wife of Mr. Jackson do anything to you?"

She didn't speak for a moment and her face quivered. " No," replied Porsche as she looked away and blinked quickly. Without meeting her brother's gaze she quickly turned around and began to walk out of the shack. She was valiantly trying to hold back tears, but nonetheless two tear drops formed and tumbled down her rosy red cheeks.

As she walked alone all Porsche could do was think about the stories of Mr. Jackson. Her longing for him to not look at her in that special way was always there. Her mind was constantly spinning with ideas of ways to make herself go unnoticed in his ever watchful eagle eyes.

Mr. Jackson waved for her to walk over to the barn. As she approached him, she could feel her heart pounding and trying to escape her body. In the distance next to the chicken coop, she saw him pick up a basket that had some red fabric hanging out of it.

"Porsche, I'm glad to see you have arrived. I have been thinking about meeting you all day," said Louis. He slipped his hand into Porsche's and gave it a gentle squeeze.

Porsche stared at him. "Are we going in there?"

"Don't look so surprised, baby girl."

"Is Mrs. Jackson here? Won't she be mad at me?"

"It's alright Porsche", said Louis. "Like I told you earlier, you are my property and I can do whatever I want to do with you."

As she began to open the barn door, she saw another male figure standing in there.

"Porsche, I have someone who is dying to meet you. This is my brother."

"It's a pleasure to make your acquaintance." As he ran his hand through her hair, he said, "My name is Javon. Louis you are right. We will have fun breaking this one in. And you are positive that her rose has never been plucked?"

" Grab that blanket out of the basket and lay it down over there ,Javon. I've got some talking to do."

"It will be alright, it will be alright," Porsche said to herself. "I can handle this. I am the property of Mr. Jackson so I must do this. Please forgive me and take my mind away from this Lord."

"Man, it has been 2 hours since Porsche has been gone. I remember her walking across the field toward the chicken coop. I bet she is sneaking some eggs out for a good breakfast tomorrow. Let me go find her."

As Raquan quietly walked across the field toward the chicken coop, he could hear someone in the barn moaning but the sound was muffled. "Wow! This is great. I bet old man Jackson is in the barn with a new play toy."

Slowly pushing the barn door open, Raquan crawled inside. At first he could only see a 6 foot man with a round belly lying on the back of a young female. Mr.

Jackson stood in front of the lady getting oral pleasure. This was the grossest thing Raquan had ever seen. He could not believe what those two old men were doing to his 15 year old baby sister. "NOOOOOOOO!" yelled Raquan. "She is a virgin." Raquan grabbed his chest and fell unconscious to the ground.

WHAT IF

ACT II

CHAPTER FIVE

USS FERGUSON 1963

"Quarters, Quarters, all hands to Quarters for muster, instruction, and inspection. Now, Quarters! Today there will be a 25 man working party. Our department has been tasked with providing 4 people. When your name is called, report to the mess decks and muster with MS1 Peterson. Seamen Jones, Seamen Crooks, Seamen Woodley, and Seamen Langston. BM1 Miller, where is SN Langston?"

"Chief, I will send someone to his rack to check up on him."

"No BM1, you will go to his rack and have him report to the GOAT LOCKER."

"SN Langston, get your ass up out of that rack. Do

you know you have missed Muster?"

" Who are you and where am I?"

"What do you mean who am I?"

" Don't play with me, Seaman. You got 15 minutes to get your uniform on. Chief wants to see you in the GOAT LOCKER. When Chief is done with you, you need to come find me at the flam locker."

As I began to approach the Door of the Chief Mess, I could see two foot print signs at a 45 degree angle and a sign that read: "GOAT LOCKER, knock 3 times then request permission to enter." My heart began to beat rapidly and the hair on my arms began to stand up.

"Why am I feeling this way? Why am I so nervous and why do I feel so anxious?"

Then, boom! It hit me. I started to remember the stories my father would tell me about how the Chief Mess ran the ship and nothing happened without their knowledge. My dad told me of an incident that involved

23

him when he was a young Lieutenant, Junior Grade. He said that because he was an Officer, the Chiefs had to do whatever he said. In my dad's mind, because he had completed four years of college this made him superior to any Chief and he did not need to knock on any door to request permission from an enlisted Sailor. He went on to tell me that one day he was looking for his Chief and he just barged on in and said, "Where is Chief Miller? I need him right now!"

Chief Miller replied, "Sir, we are in a CPO meeting and I will see you after the meeting."

"I don't care what meeting you are in. You will come now!"

At this time, the Command Master Chief stood up and I heard the door hatch get dogged down and the lights in the room went out. When he woke up he was lying on his rack. He did not know what happened or how he got there. When he went to speak to the CO and

XO about the incident, the first question they asked was, "LTJG did you knock three times and request permission to enter the Chief's Mess"?

He replied, " NO SIR," and that was when the CO and XO burst out in laughter. If my dad had learned one thing in his first encounter with the Chief's Mess, he learned to respect naval traditions.

I placed my feet on the marked spot and knocked three times. "SN Langston, requesting permission to enter the Chief's Mess."

A loud voice replied, "ENTER"

"Good morning, Chief. I am SN Langston and I am reporting as ordered. My LPO informed me that Chief Francis wanted me to come see him in the GOAT LOCKER."

As I looked around, I could see several black men sitting around a table discussing things. They were all wearing faded khaki uniforms and were holding cups of coffee. From the corner of my eye I saw a young man dressed in dark blue dress pants and a white top. He had an apron around his waist that read: "Chief's Aid". Before I could say another word a familiar face turned around. Why did he have the same features as my college professor, but only with a medium size afro and square framed eyeglasses? In his hand he held a tan colored coffee mug that had drip stains running down the side of the anchor symbol. This reminded me of my father telling me that he never rinsed his cup out in order to preserve the flavor. He would get furious whenever someone washed that cup.

"SN Langston, why didn't you make it to quarters this morning?"

Not knowing why, I quickly replied, "I overslept this morning, Chief." In the pit of my stomach I could feel anger bubbling up as I looked at him. This was the same man I just saw taking advantage of my baby sister in my dream. Was that a dream? Did all of that happen? Am I in an alternate reality? How is it possible that he is now in charge of me onboard this ship?

"Why are you looking at me with anger, Seaman?" You know if it was up to me, none of you Niggers would be in my Navy. You all are lazy and uneducated. The only jobs you are good for is preparing my meals and cleaning my ship.

"Sorry, Chief. I don't mean to look at you in a disrespectful way. I am just disappointed that I did not make it to quarters on time. I don't like to disappoint you."

"Being a suck up won't get you anywhere. This better be the last time you are late for any evolution. Get your ass to that working party and you will be on late stay today."

"Roger that Chief!" I didn't understand this. Why were there only black men in the Chief's Mess and 85 percent of the ship crew was black? Let me focus and go find BM1 Miller, I thought. What the hell is a flam locker and where is it at?

CHAPTER SIX

SAILOR'S RECOGNITION

BM1 and I met with Chief and he informed me that I needed to be at the working party today and I would also be late stay.

"SN Langston, we will be bringing on supplies today starting at 1000 this morning. Until then, I will need you to go over the side and help paint the port side of the ship. Make sure you get all of your gear. You will be working with SN Crooks."

I thought to myself that this would be an easy gig. I could simply take my time and try to figure out why I was going through this. Walking to the Boatsnmate locker, I could see this huge black man with a donut around his waist. His uniform had gray and burnt orange colors on it from drips of paint. His name tape read "Crooks". On his right sleeve you could see a small rip below his elbow. Wow! I never saw a more screwed up uniform in my life. The closer I got to him; the smell of paint thinner became more apparent.

"Crooks, I will be working with you over the side today. What and where is all the gear we will need?"

As he began to speak to me, I noticed that a brownish colored ball of tobacco was in his cheek. At the top of his teeth was a light tent of green close to the gum line with the smell of rotten eggs.

"Awa man everything is right here. Go ahead and grab one of those life jackets and a harness. Langston, I am happy to work with you. Most of the time I have to do this by myself and everyone is always telling me to shut my mouth. I don't understand why they do that to me."

"I bet if you smelled your breath you would feel the same way," I thought to myself.

"Well, I am going to need some help. I haven't done this before and you can show me."

"It's pretty simple. You just dip the roller in the pan and go up and down," replied Crooks.

"What?! No, I am asking how I put this harness on. Do we have any of them where the straps are not ripping? This shit don't look safe." I was thinking to myself, "Man, do I want him up close helping me and having to deal with his stench, or do I just want to fall into the water to get away from this nightmare? Maybe I will cut the rope so his fat ass can fall in and get a bath." I thought that the best thing to do would be to just hold my breath and hope he didn't speak to me.

"First thing you gotta do is grasp the shoulder straps and separate them. Lift the shoulder straps over your head making sure the straps are crossed in the back and

31

the harness is not turned inside out. After you do that you need to lower the harness down onto your shoulders. Take the strap and fasten the snap hook into the D-Ring for the chest. Pull the other straps between the legs from behind, as tightly as possible without crushing your peanuts."

"Damn Crooks, you know your stuff. I am impressed."

"Thanks, man. Most people be saying that I am not the sharpest knife in the drawer. I don't have a clue what they are talking about. I just smile and laugh with them. How could I be a knife and fit in a drawer? Now, let me run the safety line through the ring on your back and we can get started."

We loaded two buckets of paint with two brushes, two rollers and two pole extensions. The plan was to paint underneath the anchor first and move toward the fo'c'sle. Crooks began to sing "Anchors Aweigh" as the scaffold was being lowered. My hands were starting to grip the rope tight as the scaffold swung slightly due to the cross winds.

"Crooks, tell me a little about yourself."

"Well, what's there to tell? I grew up in Jacksonville, Florida with my 8 brothers and sisters. When I got kicked out of high school, I saw a sign that said 'Join the navy and see the world.' Well, that is why I am here."

Out of nowhere, a bell began to go off and I could hear them say, "Set Condition 1." "General Quarter, General Quarters. All hands to their battle stations. Forward, up starboard; down, aft port. There is a Class Bravo in the aft fan room. I repeat, General Quarter General Quarter. All hands to their battle stations. Forward, up starboard; down, aft port. There is a Class Bravo in the aft fan room. Now man your stations."

"Langston, what is going on and what do we need to do?"

"They are saying that there is a fire involving some type of flammable liquid. Do you remember what repair locker we should be in?

Just follow me and let's go put on our firefighting gear located in repair locker room number 3."

Crooks started to attempt to go up some stairs and boom! he caught a foot to the chest that knocked him down on his ASS.

"Hey DIRTBAG, didn't you hear them say down and aft on the portside?!!" shouted a First Class Petty Officer.

My father the Admiral taught me the acronym "FUSDAP"- forward, up starboard; down, aft, port. This means that if you need to go forward or up to get to your general quarter's station, you should move to the starboard side of the ship. Conversely, if you need to move aft or down to a lower level, you must go the port side of the ship. This keeps people from running into each other as they hurry to their stations.

"Crooks, get up! We need to go the other way. This is serious. I can see some heavy black smoke coming through the vents."

As we arrived to our stations, we could see people scrambling to put on their gear. "Langston, Crooks, hurry the hell up!" shouted Chief Francis. "Get that gear on now as you are part of the #1 firefighting party. Crooks, I want you as the Nozzleman, Cliffton and Langston you will be the Hoseman. Make sure you put on your OBAs (oxygen-breathing apparatus). NOW MOVE!!"

I could see the dark smoke starting to fill the passageway that we were in. Would I lose my life this way? As Crooks start moving forward I could feel the heat starting to intensify. All of this firefighting gear was heavy and as I moved I could hear my breathing becoming heavy. The sounds reminded me of Darth Vader from Stars Wars. Only three minutes into the firefighting Crooks fell out. As Cliffton moved up into the Nozzleman position I could see that Crooks was unconscious due to lack of oxygen. As I was holding onto the hose and pulled Crooks back, I noticed he has on the training OBA canister. Now I could see why everyone didn't like working with this dumb-ass. I quickly grabbed Crooks' tending line and gave it four quick line pulls and then another four quicker pulls. Stepping past Crooks I advanced to the back of SN Cliffton and started assisting him. Cliffton is making the fire even worse because he had a solid stream of water on the fire. I tapped him on his shoulder to switch. I switched to using the FOG technique in a slow sweeping motion to prevent scattering the fuel and spreading the fire. As the portable Aqueous Film-Forming Foam (AFFF) was delivered from the repair party, I was told to continue the process. After 17 minutes of using AFFF the fire was finally under control. Once back at the repair locker,

Chief Francis was waiting.

`"Great job, SN Langston! I am impressed with how you conducted yourself today. SN Cliffton told me how you pulled the line for Crooks and took over as the #1 Hoseman." I would have never guessed that Niggers had courage and could think for themselves. I am going to inform the CO and CMC about your actions today. Dam glad we had you down there today. You single-handedly put out the fire and saved the ship.

"Thanks, Chief. How is SN Crooks doing?"

"He will be fine. Now go get yourself cleaned up and take a break. You earned it."

The next morning we were informed that there was going to be an All Hands Call at quarters. The CO wanted to address the Ship's Company.

"Quarters, Quarters All Hands to Quarters for muster, instruction, and inspection. Now Quarters. Attention On Deck," yelled the Master Chief. The CO started to walk in front of the entire 225 man crew and followed behind him is the Command Master Chief along with the CO's Yeoman carrying award folders.

"Shipmates, I would like to say, great job on handling the fire yesterday. You proved to me that when we work together as a team all things can be accomplished. At this time, I would like to acknowledge several sailors who stood out and helped save our ship. Master Chief, call the awardees."

"Boatsnmate Chief Petty Officer Francis, Electronic Technician Petty Officer First Class Blackman, Seaman Crooks, Seaman Cliffton.. ….. Attention to Award."

The Secretary of the Navy award the Navy and Marine CORPS Achievement Medal

FOR

Professional achievement in the superior performance of his duties while serving aboard the USS FERGUSON. On June 19, 1963, you willingly entered a space that was engulfed with flames and insufficient oxygen. Taking charge of the fire hose and discharging the Aqueous Film-Forming Foam you were able to eliminate all fire, thus saving the lives of all the crew and preventing additional damage to the ship. Your exceptional professional ability, initiative, and loyal devotion to duty reflected great credit upon yourself, this command and the United States Naval Service.

Given this 20th Day of June, 1963. For the Secretary of the Navy

J. D. Smooth

CAPT

UNITED STATES NAVY

COMMANDING OFFICER

USS FERGUSON

"Chief Francis, ET1 Blackman. Post. Attention to Promotion. For noteworthy and devotion to Duty Seaman Crooks and Seaman Cliffton you have been meritoriously promoted to the next pay grade of Petty Officer Third Class. Petty Officer Third Class Crooks and Petty Officer Third Class Cliffton, Post. As the Command Master Chief, I would like to echo what the Skipper has said. You guys did great and this ship and its crew is indebted to you. A job well done. Attention on Deck."

"What the Fuck was that all about? I can't believe they did not even mention me. I was the one on the front line the whole time and they didn't do shit. None of those cock sucking black guys were doing anything. Chief didn't even show up to the scene. Oh no, I am feeling sick again."

WHAT IF

ACT III

CHAPTER SEVEN

A PROMISING LIFE

Edward Langston was a single father who worked at a social security office. His son, Jonathan, was a senior at Clark High School.

"Damn, not again, but at least I am in a comfy bed."

"Dad, Dad. I am about to head to school."

"Good morning, JJ. What are your plans for after school?"

"Dad, you know I got accepted into the University of Texas."

Edward began to laugh.

"Boy, I meant when you get out of class today."

"Oh"!

They both began to laugh.

"Well, I don't have to work today so I was planning on going to do some volunteer hours at Ronnie Turner's Assisted Living Home."

"That's fine. Remember to text me to let me know when you are headed home. BOY, pull your pants up! I don't understand why you insist on sagging your pants. You know we talked about this and how those black folks look at us white people."

"Dad, but…"

"JJ, but what? Ain't no but. Just pull those pants up on your butt."

"Yes, Sir."

"Kevin, man I am bored as shit. I feel caged up in this damn squad car. All we do is ride around these streets and see these niggers's acting like savages with their pants hanging down to their thighs and then try to run.

"Yep. How stupid are they?"

"Yeah, I know, right?" replied Steve as they began to laugh.

"Well, I can tell you this- somebody is going to get it today. I work my ass off everyday and all they do is stay on welfare colleting their dollars from the taxes I pay. My son can't even get into a college because one of them is getting grants and shit. I gotta take out loans and a second mortgage. This shit just ain't right."

"Hello, Mr. Langston."

"How are you doing, Principal Peterson?"

"I am doing fine. I just wanted to know, how is your valedictorian speech coming along? "

"I plan to work on some of it today after I do some volunteer hours at Ronnie Turner's Assisted Living Home. I should have the final draft completed by the weekend for your review on Monday."

"That is great, Jonathan. The school is so proud of

you and I know your farther is proud as well. He has raised a fine young man."

"Thank you, Sir. Let me get to my next class. I don't want to get into trouble for being late to my next class and be sent to you."

JJ and the Principal just smiled at each other as JJ walked away to class.

"Edward, I know you are so proud of your son. He will be graduating valedictorian."

"Amy, yes I am. It brings tears to my eyes to see how well he is doing."

"So, what are you getting him for a graduation gift?"

"Well, I have been saving for the last two years and I am giving him a new Mazda 3. I know he's tired of driving his beat up faded blue 2001 Integra. He works so hard at Footlocker only to have to take half of his checks to have repairs done on it. He deserves better. He never complains. I have already paid for it and once he walks across the stage I will hug him and hand him the set of keys to his new car."

"Oh, Edward! You are making me cry. That is awesome."

"Hello, Mrs. Randall. I didn't have to work today. I wanted to stop and see if you all could use some help today."

"Jonathan, it's nice of you to show up. We can always use your help."

She spoke with a sweet southern voice. The uniform that she wore reminded him of a nurse's uniform from the movie Pearl Harbor. It was all white and her nurse's hat had a ruby red cross on it. It was an old fashioned, traditional uniform and not the least bit revealing. But, the way it hugged her today was so hypnotic that he felt dizzy around her.

"The patients get so happy whenever you come by to see them. I know Alex is always talking about you."

Jonathan smiled and said he enjoys all the stories Mr. Alex shares with him about his tour in the Vietnam War and life in general.

"Jonathan, you know the rule in here. Pull those pants up on your rear."

"Yes, ma'am."

"So, Jonathan, what are you going to do when you graduate?"

"I got accepted into the University of Texas. I am here to share the good news with Mr. Alex and let him know how much of an inspiration he has been to me. After next week I won't be able to come by as often. I will be moving into a dorm room on campus soon and I know I won't be able to come visit until the next major holiday. Well, Mrs. Randall, let me make my rounds and say my good byes and I will see you around Christmas."

Click Click Click...

"Come on, turn over!"

Click Click Click…

"(713)777-9311!"

"Hello, Jonathan. How was your visit at the assisted living home today?"

"It was pretty good, but the car won't start. It is making that click, click sound again."

"Sounds like the starter again. Take that wrench and tap the starter then try and turn it over again."

"OK…"

Click Click Click.

"Still doing the same thing."

"Well, I don't get off for another two hours. You can wait for me or lock up the car and catch a bus home and when I get off I will go take a look at it."

"Yes, Sir. I will go ahead and catch the next Metro Bus. I will see you when you get home. Love you Dad."

"Love you too! See you soon. Bye."

"Man, it seems like the temperature is dropping. Better grab my Nike jacket."

It was a royal navy blue pullover with a slight rip in the right pocket. The Nike swoosh had a cotton ball color with purplish tint from grape soda being spilled on it. Jonathan placed his silver iPod in his right back pocket with the old school Scarface and Tupac hit "Smile for me" playing. "Damn it! 3:05 and the next bus pick up is at 3:17."

"Steve, it's time for some action. Look at that stupid ass Nigga running. I bet he just robbed someone and is trying to get away. Pull over and let me question him. Hey, boy come over here. I said hey boy come over here!"

As Jonathan ran to the bus stop, he could see blue lights flashing from the reflection in the 7-eleven windows. He started to slow down and took out his right hand to retrieve his iPod to shut it off. The glare of the sun hit the back of the iPod.

Steve yelled, "HE'S GOT A GUN!!"

Bang Bang Bang ….

"Holy Shit!, Holy shit!"

"Steve, I don't see a gun," yelled Kevin.

"Call for an ambulance! I thought you said he had a gun!"

"Kevin, we are gonna burn for this!"

"No way am I going down for this. Give me the throw-away from inside my bag. Get yourself together and follow my lead. The plan is that we saw him trying to grab an old lady's purse and when he saw us, he took off running. You and I saw him reaching for his gun and I shot him. Do you get it? The only way this is going to be successful is if you stick to the plan. If you don't then we both are going to fry. There is no way my children are going to be fatherless."

"Mr. Officer, Mr. Officer why did you shoot me?

I didn't do anything wrong." "Quiet down, boy. You should have never tried to pull your gun. Just relax and keep quiet. The ambulance will be here shortly."

"What gun are you talking about? I can't feel my legs, sir! I can't feel my legs! Please call my daddy, I want my daddy." Jonathan continued to say "Please call my daddy" as he passed out.

The sun began to set and it was 7:42 when Mr. Langston arrived at St. Jude's Hospital. As he pulled up, he could see a crowd of people gathered up behind barriers. Jason from the high school was there, holding a candle.

"What is going on? Why is EyeWitness News Channel 13 here?"

"Mr. Langston, Mr. Langston, can we get a comment?" asked one reporter.

"A comment about what? Let me get through to see my son. Please! Please let me through."

"Did you know your son shot that cop Mr. Langston?" someone shouted.

As I continued to walk through the hospital doors that were blocked by police officers, I could hear people shouting, "Cop Killer!"

"What is everyone talking about? I just want to see my son!"

"Mr. Langston, my name is Dr. Charles Sykes. Please have a seat and let me give you an update on the condition of your son."

"What do you mean condition? Was he injured on the bus? Why are all the cops and protesters outside? Where is my son? I want to see him now!"

"Your son was shot three times and one of the bullets is right next to a nerve that controls the lower extremities. We have been able to control the bleeding, but we need your permission to perform surgery and remove the bullet. There is a chance he may never move again."

"What do mean he was shot? When I last spoke with him he was going to catch the Metro bus home, and now you are telling me he was shot? Oh, Lord…give me strength! Can I see my son?"

Walking into the room, I could hear the sounds of air being pulled in and then forcefully being pushed out by the respirator. There was a huge tube going down his throat and two clear plastic nasal cannula slid into his nose. As crocodile tears flowed down the side of my face, I noticed that his left ankle was cuffed to the bed with a police officer sitting in the corner.

"What the hell is going on? Get those cuffs off of my son!"

"Calm down, calm down. We can talk about that later but we need to make the decision about surgery."

Holding onto J.J's hand, I could hear him breathing and his heart no longer sounded strong. I was scared he wasn't gonna make it, but I had to hold on. "Do what you must, doctor. I know the Lord will guide your hands and J.J is going to pull through this. Lord, Father in Heaven, I humbly ask that you watch over J.J and you guide the hands of the doctor as he navigates through this surgery. I ask that you do this in the name of Jesus. Amen!"

"Hello, Mr. Langston. My name is Detective Holmes. I see that you have a lot of questions and frustration on your face, but can I please ask you a couple of questions?"

" No! Let me ask you a couple of questions. Like why is my son handcuffed to his bed and who shot him?"

"The first answer is that your son was found with a gun that had ballistics matching the shooting death of Officer Cage. Officer Kevin Peters was forced to shoot your son when he tried to pull it out after fleeing from a purse snatching incident."

"What the HELL do you mean purse snatching? I

am 100 percent positive my son was not involved in any such thing. I am here to tell you that you guys screwed up. I know you all think all white people look alike. You fucking pigs claim us white people are a threat to society. You cops make me sick! I am here to let you know this is not one of the cases that you are going to pin on my son. Just because you legally pack a gun man, don't mean you have to point it at the white man. All I got to say is that you better pray my son make it through this. Get the hell out of my face!"

CHAPTER EIGHT

THE SCALES OF JUSTICE

Three months later they rolled my son out into the courtroom wearing an international orange jump suit. He no longer sported the smooth razor sharp hair line edge up. His hair was dry and prickly looking with some small dandruff falling onto his jump suit. The once cheerful and handsome looks of a young 18 year old adult had become the face of a frightened five year old boy who had broken the kitchen window while playing with a baseball in the house. I looked at J.J and thought to myself "How is this possible? My son was headed to college and now it looks like he is headed to prison for the next 25 years for something I know in my heart he has not done."

"All Rise! The Honorable Judge Ruffus J. McCane is presiding. You may now be seated. Ensure that all cell phones are silenced or they will become the property of the court."

It was not good: J.J. was going before one of the toughest judges in the city, the only judge to have a distinct look about himself. Most male judges would trim up their beards but not Judge McCane. He sported two black and gray twisted braids for his beard that resembled upside-down devil horns. His record for sentencing small misdemeanors for young white males was legendary. Last year he sentenced a 17 year old boy to prison for 24 months for stealing three cans of baby formula from a grocery store. This kid had no prior incidents or run-ins with the law. And now my only son would have to face Judge Ruffus for a killing a cop; a crime that he had nothing to do with.

"Let me make sure everyone understands this is my

courtroom and I will not tolerate any nonsense. This case will be treated like any other trial. I know the young man has already been convicted through the Court of Public

Opinion but rest assured he will be treated like any other convict...Oops, I mean, any other person on trial. Mr. Prosecutor go ahead and start with your opening statement."

"On October 17th, 2013, one of Houston's finest, Officer Cage, was on his way home when he notice a young white male running from a convenience store.

Officer Cage began to chase the member and was shot five times and left to bleed and die in the streets, leaving behind a devoted wife and three children. This case has remained unsolved until the day Officers Kevin

Johnson and Steve Brown apprehended the defendant Jonathan Langston running away from a purse snatching attempt. After he was arrested it was discovered the gun he was caring contained ballistics matched the shooting death of Officer Cage. You're going to hear testimony for the defendant legal counsel of what a model citizen he is. They will tell you about the volunteer time he does at the assistant living house. They may even attempt to bring in numerous students and teachers to speak about his positive character in school and the tutoring he did with other students. The two things that they are not going to tell you is that his prints were all over the gun that was used to kill Officer Cage. The defendant counsel is not going to tell you that he had in his possession OXYCODONE and MORPHINE pills when apprehended. And they won't tell you that he was only volunteering at the assistant living house to steal medication and make a profit off of others pain."

Oh my GOD. Listening to how they were trying to distort my son's reputation and paint him as a cunning drug dealer was sickening. Like he only went there to score drugs and not to help people. As I looked over at the two officers sitting in the courtroom, I could see the little smirk on both of their faces. Officer Johnson was sitting up tall with his chest out as he knew this is an open and shut case. My blood was boiling and I just wanted to run up there and rip his guts out.

I could hear a commotion coming from outside in the lobby. The doors swung open like saloon doors from an old western movie and a rather tall gentleman walked in and flanking him were two men who appeared to be FBI agents followed by reporters and cameramen.

"STOP!!! This trial is over!" shouted the gentleman.

Judge Ruffus began to bang his Gavel: BANG… BANG…BANG…

"Order in the Court! Order in the Court! Who are you to stop my trial?"

"My name is Special Attorney Oliver. I say again this trial is over. Agent

Carmichael and Agent Waddington take the two

suspects into custody and read them their rights."

Edward thinking to himself. What in the world is going on? What two suspects is he talking about? Jonathan is already here. I don't understand this.

"I say again! My name is Special Attorney Oliver. We have a video showing Officer Kevin Johnson and Officer Steve Brown shooting the unarmed defendant and placing the hand-gun and drugs on him. Judge McCane you have the right to be silent; any statement you make may be used against you in a trial.

We have surveillance showing that you were given the video of the two officers planting false evidence on the young man. You viewed the video and chose to destroy the copy and proceeded to conduct this trial."

I immediately ran up and hugged my son. Tears were rolling down our faces and the faces of everyone else in the courtroom.

"Mr. Langston on behalf of the Great State of Texas,

I would like to apologize for the tragedy of the ignorant prejudice of corrupt people in this world. It is 2014 and people are still judging the color of someone's skin tone rather than the merits of that person. I am so sorry that your son had to lose the ability to walk because two JERKWADS assumed he was running from a robbery or something. "

"Mr. Langston. Mr. Langston.. Hello? Hello? Are you ok?"

"Professor is it really you? What day is it?"

"Yes it is Edward. It is March 1st, 2015. You just zoned out for a minute. I remember asking you the question 'WHAT IF' and you went into a catatonic state for like three minutes. Please have a seat and relax. You act like you have seen a ghost."

"No. No. No... I am ok. I understand now. It is all clear to me now. Oh..by the way. Happy Birthday to your distant relative, Harry Belafonte."

I would like to say THANK YOU to all who have purchased and read this book. I hope it gave you an opportunity to think about what the other shoe would feel like if it was on your foot. I ask that you please take a look at some interesting facts.

2012 Comparison of Black, Latino and White Extrajudicial Killings in Five Cities

City	% of Black people in the population*	% of people killed by police who were Black	% of Latino people in population	% of people killed by police who were Latino (non Afro)	% of white (non-Latino) people in the population	% of people killed by police who were white, non-Latino
Chicago, IL	32.9%	91% (21)	28.9%	4% (1)	31.7%	4% (1)
Houston, TX**	23.7%	48% (12)	43.8%	12% (3)	25.6%	(8)
New York, NY	28.6%	87% (20)	25.5%	9% (2)	33.3%	4% (1)
Rockford, IL	20.5%	100% (3)	15.8%	0% (0)	58.4%	0% (0)
Saginaw, MI	46.1%	100% (4)	14.3%	0% (0)	37.5%	0% (0)

*Population percentages are from http://quickfacts.census.gov/qfd/states/
** The race of 4 of the 25 (16%) killed in Houston was not identified.

Drug Sentencing Disparities

- About 14 million Whites and 2.6 million African Americans report using an illicit drug

- 5 times as many Whites are using drugs as African Americans, yet African Americans are sent to prison for drug offenses at 10 times the rate of Whites

- African Americans represent 12% of the total population of drug users, but 38% of those arrested for drug offenses, and 59% of those in state prison for a drug offense.

- African Americans serve virtually as much time

in prison for a drug offense (58.7 months) as whites do for a violent offense (61.7 months). (Sentencing Project)

Take a look at the news in the so-called "kids-for-cash" scandal in Pennsylvania, in which judges took money in exchange for sending juvenile offenders to for-profit youth jails. In 2011, former Luzerne County Judge Mark Ciavarella was convicted of accepting bribes for putting juveniles into detention centers operated by the companies PA Child Care and a sister company, Western Pennsylvania Child Care. Ciavarella and another judge, Michael Conahan, are said to have received $2.6 million for their efforts. Now the private juvenile-detention companies at the heart of the kids-for-cash scandal in Pennsylvania have settled a civil lawsuit for $2.5 million. The state has also passed much-needed reforms aimed at improving its juvenile justice system and ensuring such abuses are not repeated. We are joined in Philadelphia by Marsha Levick, chief counsel of the Juvenile Law Center, which helped expose the corrupt judges and represented the families' class action suit.

Here is a look at some of the most corrupt judges in modern history.

1. *Judge Thomas J. Maloney*

Maloney was one of several judges caught up in Operation Greylord. He was caught in the act of taking bribes and even rigging murder cases.

He fixed a confirmed four cases, including a murder case, and obstructed justice during the investigation into his crimes. One of the bribes he pocketed came from political insiders with connections to the On Leong crime family. Maloney promised a not-guilty verdict for the ruthless hit man Lenny Chow.

Maloney's fee: $100,000.

2. *Judge James Henson*

Former Florida Judge James Henson was tossed from the bench in 2005 when he advised a manslaughter suspect to flee the country rather than face the wheels of justice Hanson himself was chosen to uphold.

The case involved a drunk-driving death. A judge taking on a criminal defense client is a big no-no, but advising said subject to haul-tail out of the U.S. – that's just taking corruption to a whole new level.

3. *Judge Donald Thompson*

With someone's fate on the line, you'd think judges would strive to avoid courtroom distractions. That was not the case for former Federal Court Judge Donald Thompson, who was prone to masturbating while he presided over cases of dire national importance.

He ended up being sentenced to four years behind bars after evidence was collected from under his desk and the surrounding carpet.

4. *Judge Richard Palumbo*

Maryland Judge Richard Palumbo ruled to lift a restraining order against the man who would later douse the woman who requested the order with gasoline and set her ablaze. Yvette Cade was gravely injured and disfigured.

Palumbo ignored her pleas, which were documented on tape, and released Cade's husband from the protective order. Roger Hargrave would go on to commit the unspeakable act of violence against Yvette. Palumbo was subsequently removed from hearing domestic violence cases.

5. *Judges Mark Ciavarella and Michael Conahan*

Pennsylvania Judge Mark Ciavarella is yet another man of the robe convicted of taking kickbacks. He and another Scranton judge accepted millions in kickbacks in exchange for sentencing teens to private industry juvenile detention centers.

Ciavarella and Judge Michael Conahan sentenced more than 5,000 teens to detention centers, regardless of the nature of the crimes, or whether the kids were even guilty at all. The worst kind of judge-for-sale is one that targets kids

The San Francisco Police Department (SFPD) will investigate dozens of racist and homophobic text exchanges between a former SFPD sergeant convicted of corruption charges and four other police officers, the San Francisco Chronicle first reported. The texts made public Friday included jokes about Kwanzaa, calling African Americans monkeys, calling for the lynching of all African Americans, and even one that said, "Its [sic] not against the law to put an animal down." The four officers have been on the force for at least a decade, with two having faced disciplinary action in the past. The revelation comes at a time when police practices around the country are under scrutiny for racial bias.

INTERESTING FACTS
SOURCES (S)

How Often are Unarmed Black Men Shot Down By Police?

http://www.dailykos.com/story/2014/08/24/1324132/-How-Often-are-Unarmed-Black-Me...

Information printed 3/18/2015

Criminal Justice Fact Sheet (http://www.naacp.org/pages/criminal-justice-fact-sheet

Information printed 3/18/2015

"Cash for Kids" Firms behind Juvenile Prison Bribes Reach $2.5 Million Settlement in Civil Suit

http://www.democracynow.org/2013/10/23/cash_for_kids_firms_behind_juvenile

Information printed 3/18/2015

San Francisco Cops Said it Was Legal To Murder Black

Man Because He Was An 'Animal'

http://thinkprogress.org/justice/2015/03/15/3633907/

sfpd-deplorable-racist-emails/

Information printed 3/16/2015

Top 5 Corrupt Judges in Modern History

http://www.topsecretwriters.com/2011/06/top-5-

corrupt-judges-in-modern-history/

Information printed 3/18/2015

ACKNOWLEDGMENTS

*T*HERE ARE SO MANY AND I MEAN MANY people who helped shape my life, and I would like to acknowledge some of them.

My grandparents on both sides of my family (Horton's and Smith's) were always very inspirational to me. They would often tell my brother and me of the importance of hard work and encouraged us to stay strong as we navigated through this journey of life. Thank you for taking me on many fishing trips to the ponds and showing me the proper way to skin deer and squirrels. This is where the country boy in me comes from.

To my mom and dad, thank you both for laying the foundation of versatility. Dad, still to this day I can remember you making me come out to the garage and work on cars (knowing I hated to get my hands dirty), telling me these are the things a man needed to know. Me, being the big shot smart ass I am, replied "No Dad. I will not need to know how to work on cars because I am going to work my tail off and make enough money to pay someone to work on my car." You smiled at me and said "Pass me that wrench"! MOM I am here to tell you that YOUR POWERFUL SPIRIT lives within me. I am the man that I am today because of you. I watched how you would be so kind to everyone you met and even when we did not have much you would offer a plate to a complete stranger. No matter what we had or didn't have as a family, I know in my heart that you did your very best. Thank you for taking me to the airport and hustling baggage carts for extra change. Whether you believe it not that is where my work ethic began. To my sister, cousin (Gloria) and twin brother, thanks for the love and support through it all.

My children Gabriel, Joshua, and Makayla: I

apologize for not being at some of your first rites of passage like soccer games, graduations, Gabriel's first date, and times you needed your father as you were growing up. Every day I think about how I can make my absence up to you, but know that my love for you has and will never waver. Thank you Cindy, you did a great job with our children.

To my friends who I consider my BROTHERS. Roman, Kriss, Pete, LOC, Gregg, Syko, thanks for the friendship. I took parts from each of your personalities and became a whole person. Roman, you showed me how to step my up wardrobe game when we were in high school. You and I were so different but yet the same. It is because of you that I joined the Navy. You suggested we go in on the BUDDY SYSTEM and we planned to meet at the recruiting station, but when the recruiter was driving me to go take the ASVAB I saw you and Natosha pulling into the motel. Kriss I remember you would always say "It's about the skin." The women did like to see your skin. Thanks for teaching me how to cook. The one thing I will never forget about you is when you told WENDY to turn off the lights because she did not pay no bills in my apartment and you made her sit in the dark. LOC you taught me about loyalty, and even though we may not talk much, you still remained loyal to our friendship. Gregg and Syko, there are so many stories I would like to say about our crazy encounters but I don't want put our dirty laundry out in the open like that. I have had so many fun times with you two.

Thank you to my SEA MAMA (F. TEVIS). Until I met you I had plans on leaving the Navy but you took me under your wing and my career began to flourish again. I owe the last 12 years of my career to you. The roadmap that you provided me with for a successful naval career has done me well and I have passed it on to the next generations. It is so nice to see those sailors that I have passed it on to are being very successful as well. THANK YOU, THANK YOU. Special shout out to Neal Johnson. You taught me the word HABU: Hook A Brother UP. You are the coolest black white man I know. Thank you for your mentorship as well.

To my Jacksonville, North Carolina, family, I would like to say thank you to Tonya, Kenny, Gregg, and Elva for allowing Michele and I to become part of your family. You have no idea of what an IMPACT you have had on our lives. I truly love each and every one of you.

To my buddies JP and LJ it has been great to talk with you on a daily basis. JP we would call each other in the mornings to talk about the great times in Tampa. I miss hanging out with you. Those were some of the best times of my life. Who would have thought that a FAT REDNECK and a SKINNY Brother like myself would be like blood brothers? I remember you taking me over to SLIM's house (Slim weighed over 450 pounds) and I was the only black guy there, but yet in still I was able to fit right on in with you guys. Once we left you told me never to go down there by myself because they normally did not socialize with black folks. LJ you and I would talk every day on my way home from work. I know our wives thought we were boyfriend and girlfriend since we were always on the phone. Our discussions helped me to shape my thoughts for this book and tell this story in a raw and compelling way that I hope inspires many people to look at things in a different way.

Michele, my fabulous wife, I appreciate you for reintroducing me to LOVE. You reawakened all those feeling that I had bottled up and saved me from myself. Thank you and I LOVE YOU Michele, unconditionally.